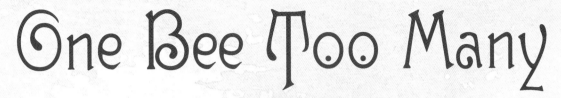

# One Bee Too Many

Andrés Pi Andreu

Illustrations by Kim Amate

Dragon Fruit

For permission requests, please contact the publisher at:
Mango Publishing Group
2850 S Douglas Road, 2nd Floor
Coral Gables, FL 33134 USA
info@mango.bz

For special orders, quantity sales, course adoptions and corporate sales, please email the publisher at sales@mango.bz. For trade and wholesale sales, please contact Ingram Publisher Services at customer. service@ingramcontent.com or +1.800.509.4887.

One Bee Too Many

Library of Congress Cataloging-in-Publication number: 2021934471
ISBN: (print) 978-1-64250-594-8, (ebook) 978-1-64250-595-5
BISAC category code: JUV012070 JUVENILE FICTION / Legends, Myths, Fables / Caribbean & Latin American

10 9 8 7 6 5 4 3 2 1

Printed in China
First printing

To Lisset Lopez, for discovering this story!
—A. P. A.

To Atena and all the little bees
that will make this mad world better.
—K. A.

One day, the bees met in the hive to discuss why they were always so cramped. They didn't have enough space to play sudoku, Parcheesi, or even checkers.

Being rather organized,
they chose three architect bees
to conduct the research.

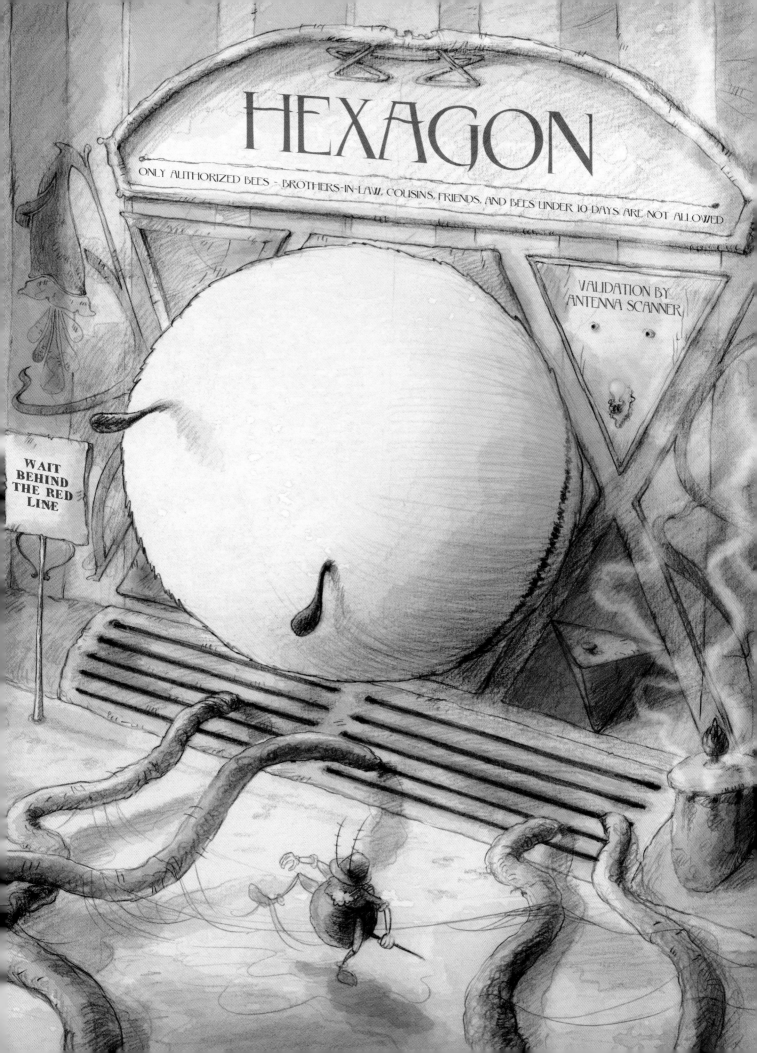

The three bees worked
day and night, night and day,
in cramped quarters—
without rest for a week.

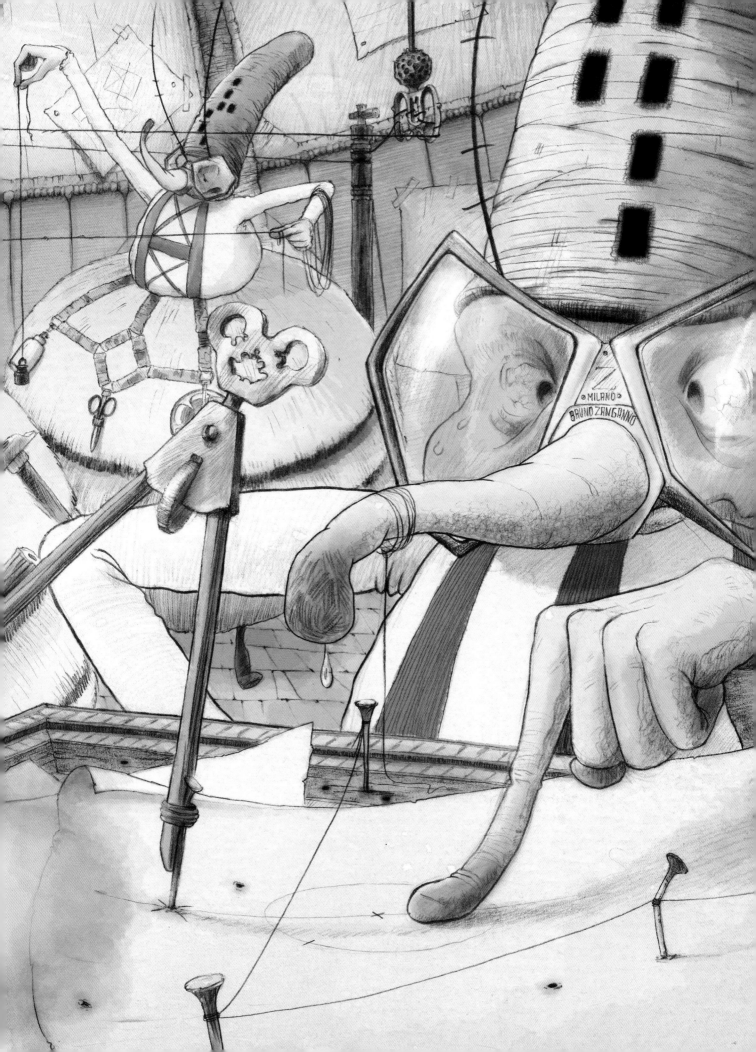

At the end of the seventh day,
they asked all the bees to gather
at the honeycomb's center.

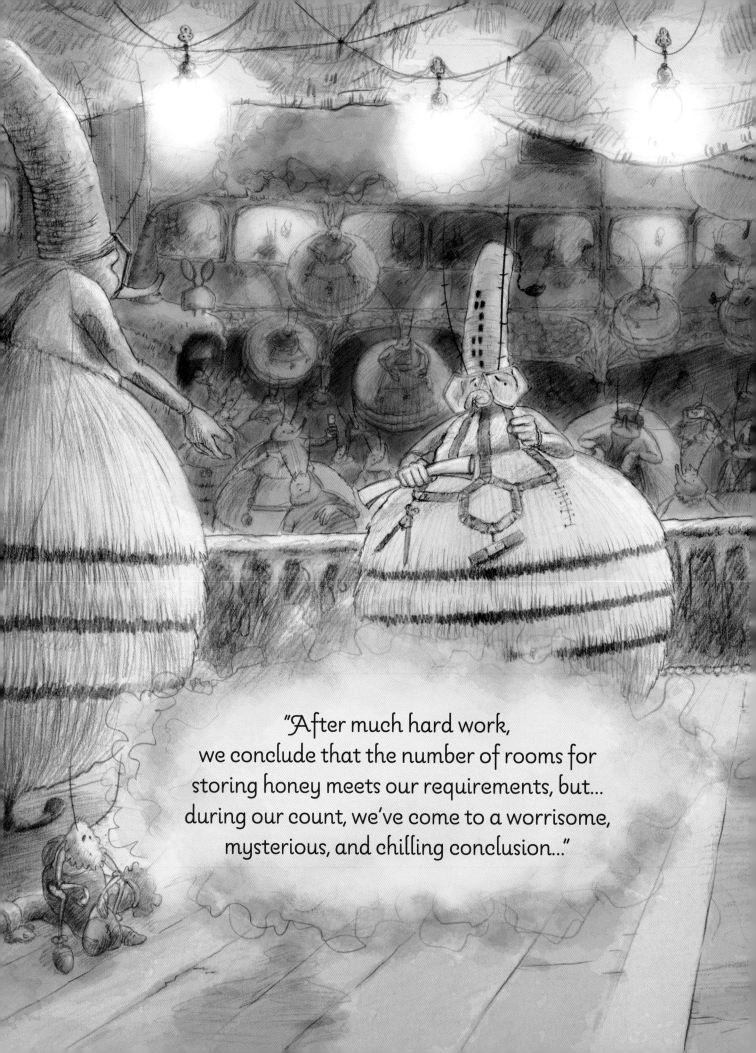

"After much hard work,
we conclude that the number of rooms for
storing honey meets our requirements, but...
during our count, we've come to a worrisome,
mysterious, and chilling conclusion..."

PULL THE
RING IN CASE
OF A BAD
SPEECH

Here, the head architect bee took
a dramatic pause, made his most
terrified bee face, and let loose,
almost screaming in hysteria:

# "THERE IS ONE BEE TOO MANY IN THIS HIVE!!!"

There was complete and total silence. Not a single buzz or drop of dripping honey could be heard.

YELLOW SQUARE

PEDESTRIAN ACCESS

"The extra bee is eating **our honey**," said a greedy bee.

DO NOT CROSS

"And it must sleep somewhere in here, wherever it can, dirty and without bathing all day long," said another.

"And who is this extra bee," they all yelled angrily, "that is taking up additional space?"

"Who is the extra bee?"
They all shouted over and over again.
"Identify yourself!"
But the extra bee did not appear.

Then the mathematician bee proposed that they assign a number to each bee. But nobody liked the idea of being the last number.

The lawyer bee suggested that they prepare passports and birth certificates.

Some supported the linguist bee's idea of listening to every buzz in the hive so as to detect a foreign accent. But all the bees buzzed in different ways.

Now the frenzy was growing and growing
into a hornet's nest of bees when
the queen, who was the oldest and most
experienced, intervened to calm things down:

"Now, friends, citizen bees,
do we not all have antennae?"
"Yes, we all have antennae."

"And do we not all have yellow and black stripes on our bellies?"

"Yes,"
replied the chorus, again.

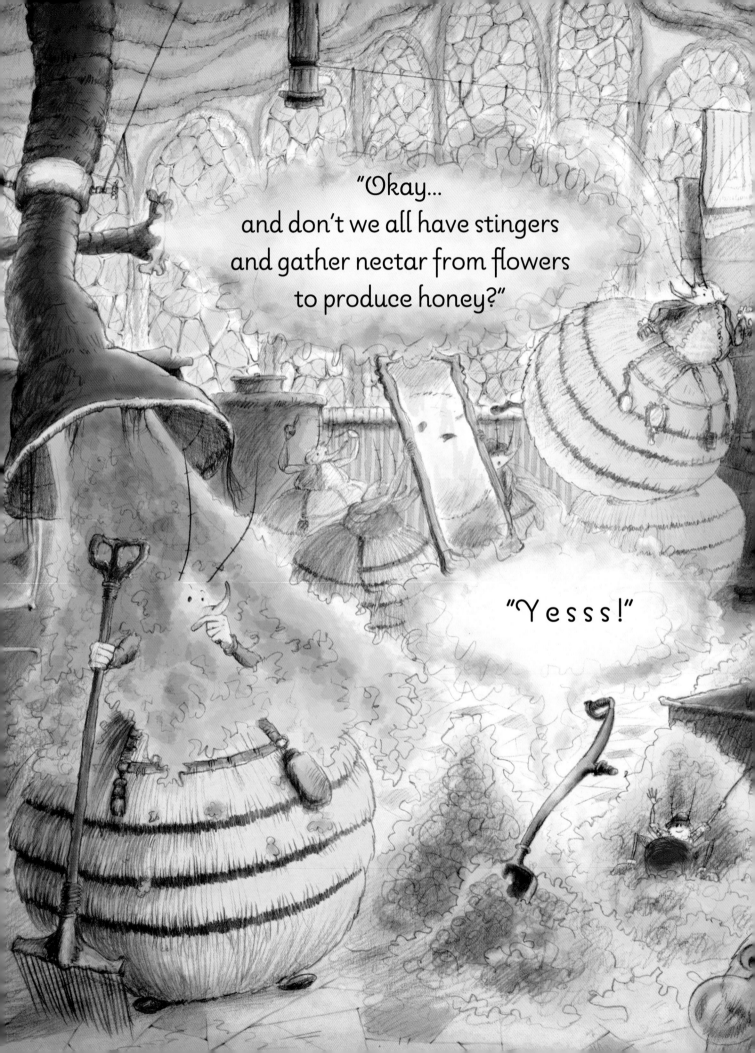

"So then, my dear bees,"
concluded the queen,
"Isn't it better to say that
our hive lacks a bedroom?"

"Yessssss!!"

responded all the bees cheerfully.
Under the direction of the architect bees,
they undertook the task of building
a lovely wax bedroom for the extra bee.

# About the Author

Andrés Pi Andreu is a Cuban-American writer, creative, and educator. With more than two hundred books published in eleven languages, he is dedicated to children's and young people's literature and has won important awards such the Campoy-Ada National Literature Award from the American Academy of the Spanish Language, the White Ravens List by the International Youth Library in Munich, the Apel-les Mestres Award from Editorial Planeta, and the White Rose Critic Award, and has been a two-time winner of the Cuban National Prize for Children's Literature, as well as Golden Age, and many other recognitions.

Considered one of the most authentic and innovative voices of children's literature in Spanish at the moment, his work is characterized by the introspection of the characters and the use of the first-person singular.

Andrés is also an innovative curriculum developer and contributing author in ELD, bilingual, and dual language education and is a National Language Consultant specializing in multimodal literacy, cross-language transference, and cultural competence. Originally from Havana, he lives in Miami.

---

# About the Illustrator

In 1974, Terrassa was a gray, industrial, and depressed city in Barcelona, Spain. Kim Amate was born there. At that time, TV shows were in black and white and that was a good thing because it encouraged Kim to pay more attention to the bugs and the books that were in the house. Later, as an adult, bored by advertising and graphic arts, he found in illustration a way of entertaining and explaining stories to curious children living in other cities with brighter TV screens and almost no bugs to observe. Their curiosity allows Kim to return repeatedly to his own childhood.

He is a 2017 Iberoamérica Ilustra finalist, on the White Ravens List, and a recipient of the Apel-les Mestres Award and Campoy-Ada National Literature Award.

DragonFruit, an imprint of Mango Publishing, publishes high-quality children's books to inspire a love of lifelong learning in readers. DragonFruit publishes a variety of titles for kids, including children's picture books, nonfiction series, toddler activity books, pre-K activity books, science and education titles, and ABC books. Beautiful and engaging, our books celebrate diversity, spark curiosity, and capture the imaginations of parents and children alike.

Mango Publishing, established in 2014, publishes an eclectic list of books by diverse authors. We were named the Fastest Growing Independent Publisher by *Publishers Weekly* in 2019 and 2020. Our success is bolstered by our main goal, which is to publish high-quality books that will make a positive impact in people's lives.

Our readers are our most important resource; we value your input, suggestions, and ideas. We'd love to hear from you—after all, we are publishing books for you!

Please stay in touch with us and follow us at:

Instagram: @dragonfruitkids

Facebook: Mango Publishing

Twitter: @MangoPublishing

LinkedIn: Mango Publishing

Pinterest: Mango Publishing

Sign up for our newsletter at www.mangopublishinggroup.com and receive a free book! Join us on Mango's journey to change publishing, one book at a time.